WHAT YOU STOLE FROM ME

Stories of trauma, resilience, and healing

SHERONE E. LEWIS

What You Stole From Me

Copyright © Sherone E. Lewis

Cover Design: Tamikaink.com

Interior Design: Michelle Boulden-Hammond

ISBN-978-1-68564-396-6

Acknowledgements

Thank you to the Lord Most High for another opportunity to share a brief part of my testimony of survival. Thank you to my family who raised me to the best of their ability and knowledge and in the fear and admiration of God. I blame no one for the trauma that I experienced. I realize that these experiences made me who I am today.

The trauma of childhood abuse, sexual assault and molestation are extremely damaging to the human body and spirit. It is possible for one to learn to persevere and to seek divine healing that nurtures resilience. I pray for those who have experienced the pain, grief and turmoil associated with sexual abuse and other atrocities; that they find hope, which is a catalyst to wholeness, that catapults us to our destiny.

Special Thanks to the Big Fella, Thompson Enterprises, Sheraya & Sweets, My Diamond Sisters, Nadine, Kim (all 3 of y'all!), Avonda, Missy, Shenika, Mia, The Life Center Family, the Preston Elementary Crew.

Peace and Blessings,

Mrs. Lewis

The author and contributors to this book are proponents of spiritual enrichment and divine healing. We encourage individuals who may have been abused (sexually, mentally, physically), who may be struggling with substance use and mental illness, to seek professional treatment and/or talk with Loved Ones (family, friends, spiritual leaders), on the journey to becoming whole.

Here are two hotlines and their corresponding websites that may also be helpful.

National Sexual Assault Hotline 800-656-HOPE (4673)
website: https://www.rainn.org/

National Suicide Hotline 800-273-8255
website: https://suicidepreventionlifeline.org/

TABLE OF CONTENTS

FOREWORD

I met Sherone in our ninth grade in High School. I was the new kid, and she was the "church girl" as I would always refer to her in my mind. There were a million differences between us, or so I thought, and later found out differently. There was one common connection, which was our love for *Martin*. The 90s television series, which featured our favorite character; you guessed it, Sheneneh! We would stand in the lunch line every day and rehearse the lines to one another and laugh and I do mean laugh.

From that moment on life took us on different journeys, only to bring us back around full circle as adults who remain friends after all these years. I am here to attest that no matter the length of time or the distance that separates, when you find a friendship that's real, you pick up where you left off last and that is how you know it's real.

Life's experiences have a way of bringing you subject to question; how would you rate the heart's condition? We reside in a cultural theme of sweeping things under the rug, men shouldn't cry, if it isn't broken, don't fix it. What happens when you get to a place in your journey and realize that you are only surviving on broken pieces? What happens when trauma and hurt begin to show up in your relationships and unmask the unhealthiness of your heart? Of course, there are things that we do not want to relive. But the journey of healing is necessary to bring you to a place where your heart's condition is one that aligns with loving yourself and the appropriation of requirements to love others in a healthy manner. This book has opened the doors of vulnerability, by only one who is truly committed to unmasking hurt and offering personal experiences. This allows God to be God, for healing and to be on a journey to the secret place that many women have experienced. Yet, many are bound by the thoughts of rejection and accusations and have made their resting place in the bed of unspoken events.I have watched this woman of God overcome obstacles, to arrive at a place where her story would awaken the healing process of acknowledgment, confession, and forgiveness. The journey of her opposition may have made her second guess her role and identity of not being enough, but that indeed has become short-lived. The strength to endure her race is one that she delves into and one that she is bent on obtaining from The Father Himself! In the words of the great Smith Wigglesworth "There is something about believing God that will cause Him to pass over a million people to get to you". Oh, what a wonderful thought this is and the same applies to you and I!

I pray that every hand that picks this book up will find the grace to overcome, to upheave, and cast down shadows and memories that have left scars that hinder the transition of trauma to the version of you that reflects healing. I know that this book will bless you as it has blessed me. Sherone my friend, you are amazing

Shenika

(aka Ms. Parker)

PREFACE

"VERONICA!!!" My mother (Chanel) exclaimed for the second time that morning. I was going to make us late for church and she was not having it. She and my sister, Cherry, were already dressed in their Sunday Best. She had started the car and was now pacing by the front door downstairs. I was almost ready. I had on a light blue dress, white stockings, and black patent leather shoes, with matching ribbons in my hair and a small purse. My Mother always dressed Cherry and I in identical outfits, especially for church.

I looked in the mirror that was on top of the wooden dresser, in the bedroom that Cherry and I shared. Mother had pressed our hair the night before. I smelled like Blue Magic hair grease and Palmer's cocoa butter that we lathered ourselves in after we took baths the night before. I still didn't have any boobs or "June apples" as my grandmother would say. I was only 11 years old, when would they start coming in? I was built like a stick, and I couldn't wait to get some hips and to "fill out" like the women in my family said I would one day.

I really didn't want to go to church. Not that I didn't enjoy church; the music, the fellowship, and an inspiring message, I looked forward to. But there was one person that I didn't want to see, Deacon Thomas. He was the lead minister and a close friend of the family who'd visit my grandparents' house at least once a month. He and my grandfather were like best friends. Deacon Thomas always made me feel queasy when he came around. He would shake everyone's hand and give me a wink, then tossel my ponytails as he walked by. His menacing smile with that one tooth trimmed with a gold cap, reminded me of the pimp in those Blaxploitation movies of the 70s. Whenever he smiled and looked in my direction with that wink, I'd turn my head as quickly as possible. The less time that I could be around him, the less that my stomach felt queasy. *Brute* cologne and a Baltimore Orioles baseball cap were part of his usual uniform.

My grandparents were outside, Cherry was with my mother. He came into the kitchen and leaned on the yellow ceramic tile countertop. I was washing dishes like mommom had asked me to. I tried to focus on the distinct smell of Palmolive dish soap, as I stared out of the kitchen window, into the back yard. Palmolive was a mainstay at my grandparents' house. It was always located atop the kitchen sink, to the left of the spigot. To this day, the smell of Palmolive takes me back to my childhood and that kitchen.

Deacon Thomas and I were alone and surrounded by the wood panel walls that graced most homes of the early 80s. He seemed to slither toward me. Before I could move, he stood behind me.

"You sure are growing up like a nice young lady".

His hot breath on the back of my neck and it wreaked of black licorice. I felt like I was frozen and that my voice was gone. I wasn't sure what he meant by that statement, but I didn't like how it hissed from his brown lips that were almost hidden by his unkempt mustache. He moved in closer, and I felt something in the middle of my back. With his rough hands, he grabbed both of my shoulders and squeezed them, pulling me back toward him.

I could hear the screen door shut, letting us know someone was coming in from the outside. He moved away and chuckled, making a remark about me doing well in school. My grandfather was walking down the hallway toward the kitchen. I could tell because he was singing a hymn and jingling his keys as he often did.

"Hey Roni girl", he always called me. "You wash those dishes good for poppop, okay. When you get done, I'll take you to get a slushie"

"Yes Sir" my only programmed response.

Why didn't I tell him what had just happened? I was so ashamed and angry with myself.

He patted Deacon Thomas on the shoulder.

"What you say there, Tom?" he inquired of my offender, in his baritone voice. He reached into the refrigerator for a soda pop. Sodas were a luxury at my grandparents' house. He enjoyed Sprite, which is my favorite til this day.

"Just talking to your granddaughter about her grades in school." Deacon Thomas responded as if he hadn't just stolen a piece of my innocence. I couldn't say anything, I had to stay in a child's place. I didn't know what to say! How could I just blurt out that a grown, married man, old enough to be my grandfather had just touched me and I couldn't explain the feeling. I would tell my grandmother; she would know what to do. At the end of the day, I told Cherry...I told Cherry everything! She didn't know what to do either. She said I was making a big deal out of nothing. Maybe I was, I should just forget about it. After all, he's a church deacon, not a *stranger* like my mother told me was dangerous, so he must be okay.

With all what Deacon Thomas brought to the local fellowship, I thought it would be hard for anyone to believe me that he was a slimy, disgusting pedophile. Although I didn't have language for his behavior when I was a child, I would guard my children from people like him, when I became a parent.

ROCK WITH YOU

(Michael Jackson, 1979)

ichael Jackson was my first crush. His curly hair, his soft voice, his dance moves, the lyrics to his songs made my little heart flutter. I thought he was so cute! Watching him Moonwalk on the Motown 25 television special, I thought he was the coolest person I'd ever seen! I knew he was a grown man, as my mother would say. I knew one day I would have a "grown man" of my own to love, marry, have children with. But until then, in my mind, I would be Mrs. Jackson and sing his songs as if he could hear me. My sister Cherry was a Prince fan. We had many disagreements about who was the cutest and who could sing better.

The innocence of a first crush can be stolen by someone that a child knows, a friend of the family, a teenager or an adult who preys on the naivety of children. As I grew up and talked with other little girls, I would ask about their first crush and when they first knew their innocence had been stolen. Often, when a little girl or boy is abused and taken advantage of, in a way that they aren't able to process it. Children usually do not have the language to express what has happened to them, especially at the hands of adults who they are supposed to trust. It was not until I saw an episode of Oprah about child abuse, heard a sermon about forgiveness and had a conversation with my college roommate who explained that she wears long sleeves because she cuts her arms to relieve the pain of abuse, that I understood some of the consequences of childhood trauma.

Growing up in Chanel's household, we did not talk about certain things. Many topics were taboo or "too grown" for children to discuss, as she would say to us. Mainly topics surrounding sexuality, but anything having to do with adults and their *grown folks' business*, were forbidden for us to be within earshot. We didn't need to know what they did for a living, where they were coming or going, if they were sick, all we knew was they "passed away and were with the Lord". Why couldn't we ask questions? Unfortunately, our curiosity would lead us to ask our peers who didn't have the right answers either.

We couldn't even say certain words that had anything to do with sex or intimacy (ex. pregnant, penis, vagina, etc.). We couldn't watch certain television shows that even insinuated what adults do behind closed doors. Cable channels were a new luxury that we didn't have access to, but it was understood that it had "bad shows" that little children couldn't watch. Wholesome television, like The Cosby Show and even Leave it to Beaver were sometimes too racy, according to my grandparents. I wanted to be just like the Huxtables; an affluent Black couple with prestigious careers, who lived in a Brooklyn Heights Brownstone, had everyday problems to solve and were raising their children to be successful. At the age of 5, I didn't realize the focus and determination that it would take to achieve such goals, especially in these here United States of America.

One of the first interactions that I can remember with a boy, outside of our male cousins, was during a Girl Scout Brownies meeting at my elementary school. We lived within walking distance of the Charles H. Chipman Elementary School. Mother accompanied us to the first few meetings, just to make sure that everything was on the up and up. By the third meeting, the other parents weren't attending, so my mother reluctantly dropped us off and went back home. I don't remember which meeting that *IT* happened during, but I do remember that *IT* happened.

The *IT* that first piqued my curiosity about boys, sexuality, and the mechanics of the "private area". During one of the Brownie group meetings, after we had our snacks, one of the Girl Scout teenage leader's boyfriends joined us in the school cafeteria. They may have been in their early 20's. I just remember thinking they were so cool and that I couldn't wait to be "a grown up" so that I could have a boyfriend and do *whatever* I want.

The guy's name was Ricardo, and all the teenage girls were giggling and gathered around him, as the Brownie's watched from their assigned seats. I thought that Ricardo was cute, but whatever those girls were grabbing at was more interesting. At one point, I looked over and Ricardo's pants were down around his ankles. The teenage girls were laughing hysterically and grabbing at the area that Mommy referred to as our "private area". I couldn't look away. There was something hanging from the private area and there was hair! What was happening?

My Mother called it our "private area" or "kitty cat", but I didn't have a name for whatever boys had in their underwear. All I knew was that whatever Ricardo had, those girls wanted it. I wondered if that was something that I would do when I became a teenager. What was the name of it? Did it have something to do with making babies? My Mother told me that mommies and daddies made babies. I think it had something to do with making babies because I also knew that Daddy had an "operation" and we had to be careful about jumping on him so we wouldn't accidentally hurt his "private area".

Although my mother would have "the talk" with me around the age of 8, my thoughts were already engaged with the incident of seeing Ricardo's private area. It was at 8 that she would teach me the correct anatomical names and tell me that those parts are how babies were made.

I remember at that age telling my mother that I wanted to be a boy. It sounded cool that their private parts allowed them to pee anywhere! She told me that God created me to be a girl, that I should be grateful, and that I would do great things when I grew up to be a young lady. I wasn't sure how Cherry felt about it, but I was excited to be grown up and to find out about those great things.

*****

The first incident that I remember, that chipped away at our innocence, was at the hands of a teenage boy, who knew better!

13

It happened while we were visiting our Uncle Bruce, who lived in North Carolina, during the Summer of 1983. Uncle Bruce was a jazz musician, and he had a gospel group called Praises Magnified.

One of those country summer days, while our mother was shopping with Uncle Bruce's wife, Alicia, James would perpetuate such an atrocity, Cherry and I talk about it until this day. Our mother had instructed us to enjoy our ice cream popsicles and to be "seen and not heard" while Uncle Bruce practiced with Praises Magnified. Uncle Bruce had created a homemade recording studio in his basement, with sponges and egg cartons on the walls. The studio had tables with huge electronic boards (hundreds of buttons, slides, and lights) and all kinds of instruments around the room. Musicians gathered every Saturday, bringing their own instruments and amplifiers, headphones, and records to sample music. The studio was filled with recording equipment, Reel to Reel, milk crates with albums, record players, tape decks and sheet music. Uncle Bruce would check on us occasionally, but otherwise, Cherry and I were content playing with our Black Barbie dolls.

One day, Uncle Bruce's friend, Mr. Johnny, brought his son, James, with him to practice. James was around 16; Cherry and I thought James was cute! I wondered if he had one of those things like the teenage girls were grabbing at during the Brownie meeting. My Mother and Aunt Alicia were having grown folk talk, so we were sent into another room so that we couldn't hear their conversation. Cherry and I went to the back porch, James was there.

He was friendly. He asked us for hugs and kissed us both on the cheek. He asked us if we had boyfriends, which made us giggle. He even asked if we wanted him to be our boyfriend. I told him that he was too old. I remember going to the bathroom and I told Cherry to come with me. For whatever reason, Cherry stayed on the porch with James. I assumed this was okay since I'd be back soon. When I got back from the bathroom, James was slouched down in a chair and Cherry was sitting beside him with her hand near his private area. She jumped when she heard me come onto the porch. I wasn't sure what was happening, but something inside told me she was in trouble.

"What are you doing?" I asked, looking from Cherry to James and back to Cherry, for an answer.

"He told me to!" Cherry explained. Her 5-year-old eyes welling up with tears.

The porch seemed eerily quiet, like a cloud of heaviness had invaded the space where we were. Little did we know that heaviness had begun to creep into our young minds.

I looked at James, confused in my seven-year-old mind. James told us to promise that we wouldn't tell anyone. What he was about to ask us to do was a *secret*. He didn't answer my question re what Cherry was doing on her knees, with her hands near his private area. He just smiled and asked if we wanted to hug him. I couldn't wrap my mind around it, but something seemed strange about him wanting us to keep a secret. I told her we should go find our mother.

The next night during bath time, my mother asked if anyone had ever touched us. In that mint green bathtub, where Cherry and I splashed in Mr. Bubble, our secret had come to the light. It seemed like she asked us out of nowhere! It was as if she already knew what James had asked us to do. As if the Holy Spirit himself had whispered to her and told her to ask her innocent daughters this wonderful question. I didn't know what she meant, so she gave an example and asked if anyone had touched our chest or private area. Her question made me feel uncomfortable, but I knew I had to tell her the truth. Just the look on my face said all that she needed to know. She jumped up from where she knelt beside the tub. Her six-foot frame leapt into the hallway and around the corner. We could hear her calling out to Uncle Bruce. Her voice was shaky but sharp. She was trying to speak so that we could not hear her. The pressure of her words reverberated around the house, from whichever room she found Uncle Bruce. I could tell that she was telling him what she suspected about James. Her words were intense, and she was crying angry tears. I could tell that she was talking with her hands, her neck was moving with every word and her hands rested on her hips in between statements.

I could also tell that Uncle Bruce was trying to console her. He left the house soon after that, I heard his Bronco leave the driveway full speed. My mother came back into the bathroom and tried to continue our routine. She dried us off, we lotioned our bodies in Palmer's Cocoa Butter and put on our night gowns. The next day was "normal", but I remember Mother telling Cherry and I that she wouldn't let James hurt us again. I wasn't sure what she meant by him hurting us. We just touched his private area, like he asked us to. I know that the following summers, although we asked about James, we never saw him again.

James taught us that boys like for their "private area" to be touched. I wasn't supposed to know what an erect penis felt like at the age of 7. He taught us that whatever a male asked us to do, we could do it without question. Without knowing it, my mother taught us that if we told her a secret, and if anyone hurt us in any way, she could make the secret and the person disappear.

P.Y.T. (PRETTY YOUNG THING)

Michael Jackson, 1982

I enjoyed learning and I loved going to school from the first day of kindergarten. My mother dressed Cherry and I in starched frilly dresses with hairbows, dress socks with lacy tops, and Mary Jane style shoes. My Mother always taught us to sit like a young lady, with our knees together and our legs crossed at the ankles. She always told us not to be "fresh" and pointed out examples of other girls who she would call "hot tails". We were to be always young ladies, but especially in public. Sit with your legs closed, don't smile a lot or grin too much at boys. If she caught us being *too fresh*, i.e., smiling at or looking at a boy too long, we would "get it".

Cherry and I always looked older than we were. By the time I was 7, I was almost 5 feet tall; I was always the chunky one of us. By the time I was 9, I wore prescribed glasses and the gap in my two front teeth would warrant braces at some point. I remember my paternal grandmother commenting that I needed some "meat on my bones". I wasn't sure what it meant but apparently, I was too skinny for her liking. But when I looked around my 6th grade class, I was the only one stuffing my bra AND wearing women's size clothes and a size 9 shoe.

Going into middle school, I towered over the boys in my class and was awkwardly up to 170 lbs. My body image concerns began during this time, as I tried to fit in with the teenage girls that I saw in the popular magazines. They were all thin with straight hair and pale skin. I, on the other hand, had thick wooly hair with copper toned skin and hips like a grown woman. I would quickly learn that Black guys like "thick" girls and that my curves would turn the heads of men who knew better.

The summer before 2nd grade, I remember New Edition had the timeless jam *Candy Girl*. I also remember my 1st kiss with my first "boyfriend", his name was Kevin. He was two grades above me in elementary school. He had skin like milk chocolate, but he also had a flat head and a crooked smile. Cherry and I were playing in the front yard while Mom fixed us lunch. Kevin dared me to meet him on the side of our house, because I was now his girlfriend. We were supposed to be playing hide-and-seek, which in teenage years became "hide and go freak". Cherry and her friends stayed near the gate at the front of the yard, like they were supposed to. Kevin and I snuck off to the side of the house to get in a few pecks, on the lips. I was so excited, my heart felt like it was beating out of my chest! Sneaking to do something that I could get caught doing became like a drug that I needed. My heart was racing because I knew at any moment my mother could peek outside to check on us. Although she had warned us about "messing with boys", she didn't teach us the good feeling of being touched, by someone our own age or otherwise. I liked the thought and the feeling of a boy wanting to kiss me because he likes me. This innocent gesture and feeling of excitement would continue into my teenage years and find me in a lifestyle of promiscuity.

One school day at the beginning of 2nd grade, I was wearing my favorite light green dress, I would experience something else that would fuel my sexual curiosity. I had a classmate named William, who I had the biggest crush on! He had caramel skin and dark curly hair, all I knew was when he smiled at me, it made my heart jump and my stomach feel queasy. We sat at tables across from each other in Mrs. Moon's class.

William didn't say anything, but at some point, he went under the table and touched my legs. Each time Mrs. Moon would turn her back toward the chalkboard, William would grin and motion with his head if I was okay with what he just did. Later that week, he went under the table and touched my thigh. As the school year progressed, he would touch under my thick cotton panties, and I would touch his private area outside of his pants. I had no clue what was happening inside of my mind and body but knew that I liked the feeling, and I would do anything to experience that feeling again. My mother had taught us that no stranger should touch our private parts. *I didn't know that NO ONE should touch me, period, especially at this young age.*

Until this day, I knew that I had a favorite dress because it had a lace overlay and reminded me of my brown faced Raggedy Anne doll. I knew nothing about a bra, besides the fact that my mother, my aunts, and grandmothers couldn't wait to get out of them when we were in the house. I knew about wearing the thick white cotton underwear that my mother made me wear. This was before Hanes or Fruit of the Loom put Disney characters on little girls' panties or superheroes on boys' underwear.

Those Summer days in Salisbury, with fresh fruits and vegetables and hours of outdoor games, festivals, friends, and family, would soon be overshadowed by my desire to feel a touch from a man or boy who "loved" me. Sliced tomatoes with dinner, family dinners during the holidays and homework should have been my focus. But the thoughts of little boys being cute and of someday being married became my primary focus. I received baby dolls for each birthday and Christmas. Cherry and I played house with our cousins, making up scenarios with false expectations of relationships. Between Sunday School lessons, soap operas and stories from older siblings, we created our own thoughts about the birds and the bees.

Apparently, William knew more than I did about those birds and bees. He knew about private parts and how to touch girls and where to touch them if he knew they liked him. I wonder what incidents increased his intrigue about sexuality. William taught me that I liked being touched. When I was touched in that private area, that must mean that a boy liked me. My Mother didn't teach us that, early enough. How William knew what to touch, I'm not exactly sure. But I am sure that some adult, another child or perhaps a movie had taught him what the "private area" was, and he learned from me that he could touch mine any time. William taught me to teach my children that there's something inside of them they feel when they experience "bad touch". I taught them that no one should touch them anywhere on their body, no matter how it makes them feel. Because at 6 or 8 years old, a child cannot fully process feelings of intimacy and sexuality.

Michael Jackson assured me at age 7, that I was a *Pretty Young Thing*. I would soon learn that there were people who didn't mean to harm me, but their warped minds and spirits, sought to damage my self-esteem and pride in the brown princess that I was.

WHEN DOVES CRY

(Prince, 1984)

Deacon Thomas was the head deacon of Mt. Sinai Pentecostal Church, everyone trusted him. They trusted him with the church offerings, with the church Mothers that needed transportation and with teaching Sunday School. My grandparents trusted him to come to their house for Sunday supper, for family events throughout the Summer or for holidays. He would often take a nap on the living room couch, recovering from what we called the "itis". The back porch is where I learned to keep *his* secret.

One day I asked him, "why do you keep touching me?"

He just stood there looking at me, grinned and winked. "Because I like to. And I think you like it when I touch you."

I felt sick and a cold chill went down my back. I really didn't know how to respond. I felt powerless, just like the other times he had cornered me in my own home. What does an 11-year-old say to an adult who's taking advantage of them? I knew he had the power, but I didn't know how to activate my power through my voice.

My entire family trusted him, that means I should trust him too, I suppose. And so began my concept of accepting that a man could mistreat me, if someone else trusted him. The next time he touched me, I hit his hand and jumped away. He looked around and reached back to grab my arm.

"The next time you do that young lady, I'm going to spank you real good". He sneered and I could see a glimpse of his gold capped tooth inside of his ugly mouth. Fortunately, this time someone came into the house and interrupted anything else he planned to do to me, in his wretched mind. He was always around, coming and going from family gatherings, as if nothing was happening.

Chanel had spanked Cherry and I a few times, for doing something or another that we knew was wrong and but tried to get away with it. The way Deacon Thomas said, "spank you", gave me the feeling that he had a different meaning. It was creepy, then the way he grinned, I knew in the pit of my stomach that he wasn't a good man. His intentions were not pure, he cared nothing about my well-being or who I would be when I grew up. Somehow, I knew that he was the epitome of evil. That what he was saying and doing to me was wrong. I also had a feeling that he would pay for what he said and did to me, if not in this life, then in the next.

*****

Although Cherry and I loved the winter holidays, which was marked by visiting our extended families, the thing that we loathed the most was going to Uncle Patrick's house. Uncle Patrick was married to our maternal grandmother's sister. He was weird, wore hearing aids, had a funny shaped head, and walked with a limp. It's not that he was weird because of how he looked or walked, but because of how he made us feel. The first Thanksgiving or Christmas that I remember visiting Uncle Patrick's house, we were forced to interact with him, which included sitting on his lap.

Their house smelled like Kerosene and wood; he smelled like musk cologne and peppermints. As soon as we walked into the house, he would grab us and hug us really tight. Although we didn't really want him to hug us, we knew not to try to push him away. This would be seen as a sign of disrespect and would

27

warrant a good tongue lashing. At some point during our visit he would ask how old we were, how we were doing in school and what we wanted for Christmas. The weirdness came when he'd say, "Come on over here and sit on Uncle Patrick's lap". Cherry and I would look at each other and try to make each other go first. We really did not want to sit on Uncle Patrick's lap. It was just something about him that we didn't feel comfortable being that close to him.

I can't remember exactly when it happened, but one Christmas, when I was about 8 or 9, I refused to sit on Uncle Patrick's lap when he requested that I do so. My grandmother was so embarrassed.

"Go ahead Roni girl," she instructed me.

I shook my head, "No ma'am I don't want to." I managed to say quietly, hot tears forming behind my eyes.

"Young lady you get yourself over there and sit on your uncle's lap!! What is wrong with you?" She said a little louder than her last instruction, this time, grabbing my shoulder and giving me a little push toward Uncle Patrick.

I stuck my feet into the shag carpet. "No ma'am. I don't want to Mommom".

"Get yourself over there!" She said, notably upset. Mommom didn't raise her voice often, so this was incredibly uncomfortable for the entire room. Poppop just sat back and watched. I couldn't make direct eye contact with him, but I could sense that he wasn't going to press the issue.

"That's okay Virgie. Uncle Patrick understands. She's getting older now." He looked over at Cherry and asked, "What about you Little One? You wanna come sit in Uncle Patrick's lap? I give you some candy." he sneered, with his cold trimmed tooth showing. There was something about his grin that reminded me of Deacon Thomas. Those hot tears that were forming, had reached my tear ducts, and crept down the sides of my cheeks. Cherry was hesitant in taking steps toward Uncle Patrick, coming past my right-hand side. Before I knew it, I had put my hand in front of her, so that she wouldn't go any closer toward Uncle Patrick. She let out a sigh of relief, put her head down and I could tell that she was crying too.

"What ails both of you?!" My grandmother exclaimed; this time seemingly more embarrassed than anything. She was reaching for her purse and motioning my grandfather to get our coats. She fussed at us all the way home, telling us how rude and disrespectful we had been. She told our mother about the incident and how they had to leave her sister's house early because of our behavior. After our grandmother left, Chanel calmly sat us down at the kitchen table.

"Are y'all okay?"

"Yes ma'am." We answered in unison.

"Can you explain to me what happened?" She questioned me.

"No ma'am. I just didn't want to sit in Uncle Patrick's lap. And I didn't want Cherry to sit in his lap either." I managed to respond, through quiet tears.

"Did he hurt you?" She asked, after she swallowed, noticeably uncomfortable.

I wasn't sure how to answer that question. It wasn't a hurt as in pain, but a discomfort and a sense of this is wrong to be sitting in his lap. "I just didn't feel like mommom should be forcing us to do something we didn't want to do." I felt bad, but that was the only truth that I could tell her.

"It's okay. Come here." She reached for me, then for Cherry. She hugged us both and kissed on the forehead. "Go ahead and get ready to get in the tub".

That night as Cherry and I splashed in the tub with Mom's Avon bubble bath, we tried to make sense of what happened. Although we didn't understand why we didn't want to sit in Uncle Patrick's lap, we were both adamantly against it. We both agreed that if one of us didn't want to do something, we would stand up for each other.

I can't say for sure that Uncle Patrick touched us. But I knew it didn't feel right for us to be sitting in this man's lap. I vowed that my children would NEVER sit on anyone's lap. Whether they be male or female, family, or friend, and definitely not-if they are a stranger (ex. Santa Clause).

*****

By the time I was 12, I began to understand the power of my *lips, hips,* and *fingertips.* You couldn't tell me nothing! Those "June apples" that my grandmother said would come in, had blossomed. I had discovered padded bras and stretch pants were all the rage. I found that middle school boys didn't think I was cute and didn't really appreciate my curves. Unfortunately, Deacon Thomas didn't miss the young lady that I was blossoming into. One day he asked if I had "gotten my cycle yet". I knew it was none of his business, but I told him yes anyway. Shortly after that, he left me alone. Classic traits of a pedophile.

To Dondre, Dominique and whoever else I had a crush on in middle school, I was *the homegirl*. LL Cool J had a song that reminded me of myself, called Around the Way Girl. My mother didn't buy us name brand clothes or expensive shoes. She was practical, sensible, and most importantly, she was on a budget. As teenagers, Cherry and I shared clothes and put together outfits the best we could. We weren't allowed to wear flashy jewelry and our makeup was to be modest. Big earrings and red lipstick were for fast girls and loose women; at least this is what we were taught in sermons and in Sunday School lessons.

Like any other teenager, I struggled to "find myself, to find my voice, to fit in with my peers and to establish myself within my peer groups. For minority teenagers, this struggle is often compounded. How do you get established when your peer groups don't look like you, aren't in the same socioeconomic status as you or don't share the same faith as you? How do you feel when you watch Rodney King be beaten by police officers who are supposed to *protect and serve*? How do you determine where racism fits in the doctrine that's preached every Sunday and taught during Wednesday night Bible studies? What if it's not addressed at all, but you become within yourself as you sit in a class of 20 students but only two or three of your peers look like you?

I found myself with so many unanswered questions and feelings of inadequacy. There wasn't Google or access to any other search engine. Anything we wanted to know that my mother didn't have the answer to, she would refer us to the expensive set of Encyclopedias that she purchased through monthly payments. I never found the section in the library on how to confront racism in school. Nor did I find what to do if you're always around someone who's actively molesting you at least once a week.

I cried and prayed but I wasn't sure who I could go to and share this pain that I experienced at the hands of a trusted family friend. I began to feel guilty about him touching me, so I found ways to avoid him and made sure I wasn't alone with him. I found a replacement for those feelings that I first had in elementary school, of wanting to be touched. Food became my new drug. A slice of cheesecake, a Snickers or some French fries seemed to numb the pain and guilt and I continued to hide those feelings from one boyfriend to the next.

Deacon Thomas passed away when I was 16. A few months after he was eulogized and buried, I told my mother everything he'd done to me. She was distraught and disturbed that I hadn't told her when it was happening. With tear filled eyes, she apologized for not knowing and not being there for me. It was then that I understood parents make mistakes too, they aren't always right and it's okay to apologize to your child when you are wrong. To this day, I don't know if my mother ever told my grandparents that Deacon Thomas had molested me from the age of 8 until I was 13. I know it would have crushed my grandparents to know that their trusted *head deacon* was a pedophile. They were married in their teens and raised children during the Jim Crow age but couldn't talk about sex or relationships and they still referred to themselves as Colored. We couldn't even say the word pregnant around them, they only spoke of women being in "the family way".

If ANYONE had asked me if Deacon Thomas had touched me, I would have told them the truth! The problem was, they expected me to come to them with my secret. It usually doesn't work that way. Cherry had experienced these incidents also, but not to the degree that I had. We went to his funeral, to keep appearances; everyone knew that our families were close. My secret died with him. His wife and 5 children would never know. I wondered if he had ever touched any of the other girls at church or my cousins or any other little girl that he wanted to touch. I didn't learn until I studied psychology in college that he could be diagnosed as a pedophile.

Being a survivor of molestation, taught me that I could hold secrets at the cost of my own pain. And that I could move on to the next "relationship", which would distract me from healing that pain. Do doves really cry? I suppose that Prince was singing about a consensual adult relationship. But the pain that I endured and carried for decades, created a trail of internal tears that only God could heal.

LET THE CHURCH SAY AMEN

(Andre Crouch, 2011)

"**V**eronica Evette!! Get your hindparts down these steps before I come up there to you!!" My mother exclaimed from the front door.

I must have missed the first two times that she called me. I could tell this because her use of my first AND middle name, which meant that she was frustrated and waiting on me. I snapped out of my daydream, grabbed my patent leather purse, and skipped down the steps of my childhood home. I tried to pass by her, but she was standing in front of the coat closet that I needed to get into. I knew before I stepped out of the front door to get into our brown Plymouth and head to church, I had to get the final inspection from my mother. She would make sure my hair had no fly aways, that there were no "runs" in my stockings and no scuffs on my patent leather shoes.

Sundays were always a big deal for our family, from the programmed church service to the Sunday evening meal. My mother and father were both raised in the church. Each Sunday we were paraded through Sunday School, Morning Service, Afternoon Service (at a different church) and maybe Evening Service back at our home church. Then there was Tuesday Night Bible Study, and Friday Night Fellowship Service to support the Brotherhood, the Usher Board or Young People's Committee. As an adult, I came to realize that all those services taught me discipline, to be consistent and to be a woman of my word. I would raise my own children in the church, teaching them to honor the Lord. I wanted them to learn Biblical principles but also to find their voices and to speak boldly about what they understood of the Holy Scriptures and personal relationship with Christ.

Every three months our church would gather to fellowship with other churches in our district council of the second largest Pentecostal organization in the world. Cherry and I would be so pressed to see our friends from D.C., Delaware, and other parts of Maryland. The Council meetings took place at larger churches and then at hotels, as the attendance grew to thousands. We looked forward to the preaching, youth services, the combined choirs, and the new clothes that we adorned for these special occasions. The Council always energized us to return to our local churches with the ideas that we could implement at our local assemblies. We also took it as a chance to see what the city churches had, new songs that our home choir could sing, not to mention new hairstyles and fashions that hadn't yet come to the Eastern Shore. My grandparents shared stories of the Councils when my mother and her sisters and brother were younger. The format and order of the organization had remained, but outside influences ripped away at the core moral goodness of what the organization was supposed to stand for. Although our local church congregation was small, we loved the intimate fellowship and the responsibilities that we had as the Pastors grandchildren.

My maternal grandfather was the Pastor of Mt. Sinai Pentecostal Church for 32 years, until cancer was too much for his body to sustain in the pulpit. He was a no nonsense, stern looking man who I came to realize was a gentle giant. He was born at the end of WWI, lived through the Depression, pressed through Jim Crow laws, viewed first-hand the riots of the 1960s and free love of the 70s. He shared few details about his growing up and all that he endured, but you could tell by the worry lines across his forehead, that he had many stories to tell. Six feet tall, dark brown skin, hardened by years of working in the sun. I remember he had rough hands that cooked huge pots of beef stew, cleaned HVAC systems, and chopped logs for the woodstove that graced the kitchen. My maternal grandmother was the Church Mother, respected for wisdom and rebuke when necessary. My paternal grandparents lived within 20 miles of my childhood home. They were also pillars of their church and of the community. They had raised their children and fostered more than 40 children in their home. When Cherry and I came along, we had more aunt and uncles than we could stand. They are part of the family, each with their role in our lives.

*****

Until I went to middle school, I was shy and very soft spoken. Chanel sheltered Cherry and I against the wilds of the world. She took literally the Scripture that we should be in the world, but not OF the world. We did normal things like play with toys and watch TV, but we weren't allowed to wear certain clothing, we couldn't listen to anything but gospel music, and we weren't allowed to attend any churches outside of the ones we fellowshipped with.

One thing that I knew for sure is that I loved church! I loved the feeling that I experienced when we praised the Lord. We were what some may call charismatic, we called it Pentecostal. We danced, sang, clapped our hands and lifted up the name of the Most High God. Unfortunately, there are always secrets within families, including the church family. Whether those families are spiritual, blood or friendships, some secrets must be told.

By the time the Council meetings moved to convene at hotels, Cherry and I had part-time jobs and we got permission to stay overnight from the Thursday night to the Saturday night events. The Council meeting after my sophomore year in high school, Cherry, our cousin Michelle, and I did just that, we got a hotel room. Because of our influence with music by Uncle Bruce, we seem to be drawn to Musicians. I loved and still LOVE music. All types of music, from gospel to Go Go and classical to country. Although I had to sneak to listen to these other types of music, when I heard them, I was delighted with their riffs, rhythms, and instrumentation.

Maxwell and his crew were the musicians for a church in Baltimore. They could each play the keyboard, bass guitar and drums, depending on the song that was sung. As usual, we had picked out our best matching outfits. Nothing spectacular, just something we could afford, from the nearby Rainbow or Fashion Bug. We hadn't stayed in many hotels at that age, but we knew just enough to check in, hang up our clothes, dress in those matching outfits and flounce around with Maxwell and his crew. That Thursday night, we staked out the guys that we liked most and told them which hotel room we were in. That Friday, we hung out in their hotel rooms, giggling, and listening to stories that were fresh to our naive ears. They were nice, offered us food and promises of what they could offer us young teenagers. We had the time of our lives! No adult supervision, just living our best lives, in the company of cute men, with no rules. I left that hotel still a virgin. For some reason, this was a big deal and a few of the crew members wanted to "pop my cherry". I had no intention of giving my virginity to some guy that I didn't know.

On our way home to Salisbury, I could tell that Cherry was different. She was smiling, but something (or someone) had changed her. I couldn't put my hand on it, but she mentioned during the car ride that she had something to tell me. Michelle on the other hand was an open book. She told us in detail about each of her excursions with grown men, in different hotel rooms. Michelle was definitely a wild card!

When we got back home to the Salisbury, Cherry told me about how Maxwell seduced her and performed numerous sexual acts with her; he was 20, she was only 15. Maxwell did things to her sexually that would change her sexual appetite. Maxwell teased and tantalized her teenage body to the point of no return. He introduced her to a world of seduction and perversion that her naive mind wasn't prepared to receive.

If only the church folk had discerned the likes of Maxwell and what he desired. Instead, they looked at his gift (which was without repentance) and assumed he loved the Lord, so he was okay to play instruments at their churches and make the people dance. What if Cherry had told the faithful church members about her excursion with Maxwell, would they have blamed her? Would she be known as the church whore? Would he be scrutinized or condemned for his thoughts that lead to his despicable actions?

Church taught me that the worst secrets were kept by those in "the house of the Lord". That *church people* could gossip the most about each other, they didn't really like each other yet they smiled in each other's faces and that they were "going to heaven" no matter what. Although I hoped that by growing up in the church, I would have been taught more about scriptural application, I am certainly grateful for the foundation of the church. Knowing Scriptures, hymns and spiritual songs and the discipline of attending services regularly is certainly ingrained in me now as an adult.

WEAK

(SWV, 1992)

The Summer before my Junior year of high school, I became a woman! Or so I thought. Most of the girls in my class had given away their "V card" somewhere around prom time. I didn't go to my Junior or Senior Prom. Chanel gave me permission to go, but the church spoke against us going, because they would be playing *worldly music*. My friends giggled as they shared stories of their primitive, amateur sexual exploits in small huddles and in intricately folded letters passed around during 3rd period. There were a few of us who had boyfriends and talked trash about our "sexual skills", but we still hadn't officially had intercourse yet. Being the "good, clean church girl", I was certainly curious, but I didn't want to give my virginity away to just anyone! I had really convinced myself that I would wait until I got married. But as the attention (from teenage boys and old men alike) grew, I wondered what it would be to be held and to experience making love. My naivety and curiosity convinced me that I could just "do it" once, to quench my thirst. What could it harm? I would be careful and make him wear a condom. I would just tell my circle of a few close friends, so I wouldn't be known as a hoe.

In the summer of 1992, Cherry and I went to Uncle Bruce's, as usual; he lived with his wife in North Carolina. Uncle Bruce lived in what they called the suburbs, with nice, manicured lawns and middle-class families who worked in jobs having to do with finance or state. He had two extra bedrooms, one that my Aunt Mary had turned into a sewing room. That summer, Cherry and I claimed the third bedroom and den as our domain. When we would visit Uncle Bruce and Aunt Mary as children, we'd stay for maybe a week and our mother would be with us. We made friends and played in their yards as the old folks prepared cookouts with Colt 45 and music from Radio Shack sound systems. *Summertime* by DJ Jazzy Jeff and the Fresh Prince was in full force and became my anthem of the official start of Summer. SWV had just hit the mainstream with their uptown, R&B vibe. I loved their sound and their style of clothes;

also, they could REALLY sing! By the end of the summer, I would understand the true meaning of being *weak in the knees.*

My first real teenage boyfriend was Daniel. We met at a Thursday night basketball game where he attended school, in Delmar, MD. My friends dared me to walk up and start talking to him. He was dorky, lanky, he wore glasses, and he wasn't athletic like the ideal guys that most teenage girls were attracted to. When I found out he had graduated from high school already, I was up for the challenge of keeping his interest. He was 19 and I could easily pass for 18. We didn't have sex but we "fooled around", and I do mean A LOT. Heavy touching and kissing were always involved during our time together.

When Daniel touched me, it was different than when Deacon Thomas had touched me. The difference was that I really wanted Daniel to touch me, and I was now mature enough to process what his touch meant. He had a part time job at Food Lion, he could borrow his parents' car, and he could close his bedroom door when I went to his house.

When I turned 16, I was officially "hot in the behind", as my Aunt Marie and Aunt Christine reminded me of often. Although I learned about fornication and what the Bible said about having sex before marriage, I had an urge that I couldn't explain. I believed what the preachers said and what my mother warned me about, but I didn't know how to not think about the *forbidden fruit* of sex. No one explained to me how sin made The Father feel about his creation. Yes, The Father loves us regardless, but He is also grieved by our sin. They just said, "don't do it and you'll go to heaven". No one taught me about discipline, as it relates to food, time, or financial stewardship. Sure, I could have done my own studies and searched for a better understanding of Christianity. I wouldn't know to do this until I went to college.

*****

That Summer, we went to stay with Uncle Bruce and Aunt Alicia. My mother needed a break from the teenagers who now invaded her house with bad attitudes, boy talk and "eating up all her food". The first night of our stay in Raleigh, Cherry and I reunited with our childhood friends: Shanda, Asim, Ronald, Omar, Denise, Sharina, Cynthia and of course, Bryan. Sharina and Cynthia were a few years older than us and knew more about the ways of the world. They sort of took us under their wings, teaching us about boys, the latest styles, and the best music. Bryan gave me a quick "hey" and diverted his eyes quickly, to not appear "pressed". By the end of the first week, we were all hanging until our curfew, in the cul de sac or at the basketball court outside of Sharina's parents' house.

Bryan worked at Popeye's which was at the strip mall in walking distance. Cherry and I walked there often, using the allowance that Uncle Bruce gave us for doing chores around the house. By the third week of our stay, Bryan was "picking with me". He was making comments about how big my butt was and asking for a hug each night when I had to go into the house for curfew. July 4th was our first "date". He used his mother's car, and we went to see *Boyz In the Hood* at the $5 movie. Bryan was like the character 'Tre'— smart, cute, and not trying to be "hard" to impress his friends. Each week after that, when Bryan got his paycheck, we went to see a different movie at the $5 movie place, this way he could splurge and buy me a soda, some popcorn and candy (Jujubes were my favorite). The type of movies that Bryan liked, New Jack City for example, exposed me to a lifestyle that I hadn't seen or experienced on Maryland's Eastern Shore. I'm sure that remnants of the Crack Epidemic were all around us; Chanel kept us well secluded from drugs and we were from the "Just Say No" era.

By the fifth week of Summer, it was official, Bryan and I were "going together". I knew that back at home, there was Daniel, but he was my school boyfriend. Bryan and I could be summer buddies. Cherry would keep my secret with that. The problem with this mindset is that mentally you think you're playing the guy, but he's playing you too! Bryan didn't really talk about sex, but his roaming hands let me know that he wanted to explore the forbidden parts of my body. My body reacted to his soft tender touch, and he was a much better kisser than Daniel.

One day when he didn't have to work, Uncle Bruce would be gone late into the night and I was so curious and 'hot and bothered', I decided to pay a visit to Bryan's bedroom. I didn't usually go into his house at all. Our parents were alike in that they didn't let any of their children's "lil friends" hang around inside their house. This one day, I had this feeling in the pit of my stomach that my time with Bryan would be life changing. I knew that he had had sex before and he very well knew that I hadn't. For whatever reason, I went to his house very early, and he was still in the shower. When I heard the shower turn off, my stomach dropped as he walked out of the bedroom, almost in slow motion. The water droplets that cascade down his chocolate skin were almost calling me to rub my hands across his chiseled chest. Unlike Daniel, Bryan had curly hair and a smile that only Billy D. Williams could match. He saw me admiring his muscles and gave me a wink. Instead of getting dressed, he walked over toward where I was sitting. His stare made me uncomfortable, and before I knew it, he had cupped my chin and was kissing me gently. Although I responded to his advance, he stepped to make sure I was okay with what he was doing. I always appreciated that he waited for my response, and he made sure I was comfortable with whatever he was doing. He gently pushed me back on the bed and motioned if he could pull down my shorts. He stopped mid motion and went to his Casio stereo. Honey Love by R. Kelly began to play softly. I smiled and rolled my eyes; he KNEW that was my song!

What proceeded next could only be described in a Music Soulchild song. Bryan was so sweet and took his time with me. It wasn't anything like the vulgar and often scary conversations that my classmates had shared about their sexual experiences. Nothing like the sexual exploits in the movies either! It was as if Bryan responded to every desire that my body craved. I felt a different connection with him, after I left his bedroom that afternoon. He made me lunch and held my hand as he walked me back to Uncle Bruce's house. I walked differently, I smiled differently, and I couldn't wait to see him again so that we could enjoy each other more.

That summer taught me that there was love to be made, even if I felt guilty the next Sunday at church. I can't say that I loved Bryan, but when I saw him the next summer, we picked up where we left off.

SWV said it best. *"Cause my heart starts beating triple time/with thoughts of loving you on my mind. I can't figure out just what to do, when the cause and cure is you!"*

HONEY LOVE

(R. Kelly and Public Announcement, 1992)

Giving away my virginity was the beginning of an uncontrollable appetite for sex, spanning over two years. I was in an addicting spiral that I didn't understand. I slept with several men during those years, ranging in ages from early twenties to almost 30. What had I gotten myself into? I began to lie (to myself and to others), cheat and to engage in sexual activities as if I had no morals or values, no self-esteem, or no boundaries. I was going with the false perception of what love was supposed to feel like. I wanted to feel what I felt with Bryan, and I began to seek it out, like a drug addict.

I began my junior school year with Daniel as my boyfriend, as if I hadn't had sex (numerous times) with Bryan, over the Summer. Daniel was none the wiser, until he and I had sex for the first time. He was a Senior, so we looked forward to Homecoming in the Fall. Daniel was the perfect gentleman, we went to the parade, the homecoming game and dinner after the Homecoming dance. Our matching outfits, black and gold were a highlight of the event! That weekend, Daniel's parents were out of town. It had been an entire month since I had sex, and I was curious about Daniels' capabilities. Could Daniel make me feel like Bryan had? I just wanted to feel wanted, special and desired. Daniel didn't give me that feeling, like Bryan had made me feel. I wanted Daniel. I needed him to want me and to make me feel like Bryan had.

Before the Homecoming dance, I suggested heavily that I wanted to lose my virginity with him. After the dance, we parked at the marina, near the Salisbury Zoo. Under that clear starry night in October, I wanted Daniel to make love to me, sweetly, gently and to satisfy the urge that I now had, after being with Bryan.

That night, I tried to guide Daniel, his hands, his kisses, to do to me what Bryan had done. It didn't feel the same. At some point, Daniel leaned back, turned the inside car lights on and looked at me. In the awkwardness of his 1990 Ford Taurus, the look on his face had questions. Questions that I didn't want to answer and would be ashamed to answer. He put his hands over his face, looked back up at me and asked me that question that I dreaded.

"Have you had sex before?" he asked me, in an almost whisper.

One thing I didn't want to do was lie. After all, I was a "good clean church girl".

"Why would you ask me that Daniel? You know that I love you!" Tears came from somewhere. Not from an honest place, but from a place of remorse for what I had done to my boyfriend.

He apologized and explained that he felt like something was different. I told him about Bryan, not everything about him, but enough to clear my conscience. I told Daniel that we went to the movies, and we hung out, and that it was just something to do, to pass time during the summer. He believed me. I was believable—the good clean church girl that I played the role to be. We did have sex that night. It wasn't good. Not good like Bryan. I wasn't fulfilled. There had to be more!

I sat in Sunday Service, guilty as a sinner on judgement day. Oh wait, I was a sinner, who believes there will be a Judgement Day. Who could I tell, besides Cherry? I felt that the Saints were judging me. I felt like my mother knew. She began to share stories with me, about her boyfriends as a teenager. Not in a judging manner, but just to say, we all make mistakes and that she wasn't perfect either, growing up.

Daniel broke up with me before that Thanksgiving. I was sad, but I wanted to replace him with someone else soon, because I hated the thought of being alone. Daniel and I were high school sweethearts. He told me that he liked me at Homecoming my freshman year. I couldn't believe that I messed up my first long term relationship. Daniel was so kind and respectful of me wanting to be a virgin. And I repaid him by cheating and giving my virginity to someone else.

*****

Right before Christmas, Jude came to visit my grandparents' house for a family dinner. He was a friend of the family; he came to visit us when Uncle Bruce came into town. I could tell that Jude was checking me out, but I ignored him because he was almost 30. He kept trying to make small talk, asking if I liked school, what I wanted to be when I grew up and if I had a boyfriend. I answered his questions, but his last question, and the way he gave me the up-down while grinning, was all too familiar.

He wasn't cute and I wasn't really looking for a 30-year-old boyfriend. He smoked cigarettes and always had a beer when he came to visit (he and Uncle Bruce used to drink outside). Why would Jude be interested in me? He could have a girlfriend his own age. He came to visit again after the new year, this time with more questions. I tried to avoid him, until he started flirting with me. He complimented my outfit, he made comments about my physique and told me that I had a nice smile. I was curious. What if he could make me feel like Bryan had?

Jude started making excuses to come over to our house more often. He was a handyman and offered to do things around our house. Chanel stayed close to him, making sure he wasn't doing anything inappropriate to her Cherry or me. About the fourth visit, I started responding to Jude's advances. He challenged me, my womanhood, or who I thought I should be as a young woman. I told Cherry just in case something went down.

Close to Valentine's Day, I met Jude at the strip mall near our house. He had a red FordFestiva; it was a stick shift. I was wearing a plain white t-shirt and a pair of black biker shorts. This was my 'I know I'm cute' outfit. I knew that Chanel would flip, if she knew where I really was and what I planned to do. When

I got into his car, the first question he asked me was if I knew how to *drive stick*. He had his hand on the gearshift, but the sneer on his face let me know he wasn't talking about driving a car. I grinned wide and rolled my eyes, turning my head so that he couldn't see me blush. He asked where I wanted to go; I had no clue. I knew that he had an apartment, as any 30-year-old man should.

I didn't know much about Jude, like where he worked, where he went to school or even where his apartment was located. He lived in a nearby town called Princess Anne. He drove down the backroads from Salisbury to his apartment, to avoid any contact with anyone we both knew. We chatted about this and that, but mostly he asked questions about my "sex life". I really didn't have a sex life, but I fed into his questions, making up stuff as I went along. I found that I liked to talk trash, even if I didn't know what I was talking about. Jude liked my responses; I can tell by the way he smiled and continued to challenge me.

Over the next two months, every time Jude asked me to see him, I would sneak out, lying to my mother and others. And most every time, we'd have sex. Because he had his own car, we had sex at his apartment, or in his car in random parking lots. Once we even had sex outside of his aunt's house, after he invited me to meet his cousins. He lied and told them that I worked with him part time at a shipping fulfillment place. Our cover was almost blown, because one of his cousins went to high school with my mother. He was a good liar, so he made up something to cover his tracks. He had even told them that I was 19. They all just shook their heads and looked at me, wondering why a thirty-year-old man was with this young girl. No one asked any questions, although I wish they had.

Jude taught me everything I wanted to know about sex. He showed me different positions, taught me about my own anatomy and taught me how to use my body to best please him sexually. He had a collection of pornography-VHS tapes at his apartment. Every time I would visit him, we'd usually watch a tape to get him started. He was a good kisser. He would grope and handle my body in a way that I wasn't used to. Daniel and Bryan paled in comparison to what Jude taught me. I wasn't really attracted to him, but the level of sexual expertise that he had was priceless! We weren't intimate; he didn't hug me or hold my hand or anything. After we kissed, he'd just start taking off my clothes and *it was on!*

My relationship with Jude (if I can even call it that), left me empty. Sure, I could say that I was having sex with a grown man, but what did it bring me but a sexual skillset that I could have learned in intimacy with my husband. I couldn't tell my friends and brag like my other peers during school. I knew that what he was doing with me was illegal. I also knew that he didn't love me. I think he was just having sex with me to have bragging rights with his friends, whom I never met. We didn't have any meaningful conversations. He didn't talk about God, finances, future goals, or anything else of any substance.

Being with Jude made me think that love was the same as having sex. I could have any man I wanted, by allowing him into my intimate space. That if I knew how to do different tricks and to give a man what he liked, he would love me. Jude never told me that I was pretty, smart; he didn't compliment me at all unless we were having sex. While he was inside me, he would tell me how good I was and how he wanted and needed me. In the heat of the moment, I liked hearing those "compliments".

None of the male figures (blood relatives or church leaders) that I was raised by, told me anything positive about myself. They didn't validate me or reassure me that I was someone valuable in this world. Maybe they didn't know that I needed to hear that I was important, that I could make a difference, that I was pretty, smart and could be anything in this world that I wanted to be. Maybe they didn't have the capacity to tell me reassuring affirmations that every young person needs to hear to solidify their identities. If none of the male figures in my life hadn't been told by their parents or family members, how could I have expected to hear it from them.

BOUNCE, ROCK, SKATE, ROLL

(Vaughan Mason & Crew 1979)

That Easter, I had stopped sneaking to see Jude regularly, but we hooked up that summer a few times and then I cut him off. We went to Aunt Marie's apartment for Easter Dinner. She lived outside of Washington, D.C., in a city called Seat Pleasant. Aunt Marie didn't have children of her own but loved Cherry and I as her own. We went there Saturday afternoon, for the meal preparation. Our Easter dinner menu included baked ham, fried chicken, collard greens and cabbage mixed, potato salad, rolls, and iced tea. The guest list was my mother and Cherry of course, my maternal grandmother, Uncle Bruce, and Aunt Christine. I loved our holiday family dinners. Listening to their stories from back in the day. Helping with the meal and learning family recipes.

Miguel was a guy that we knew who lived near Aunt Marie's house. Cherry and I hadn't seen him in a few years. I thought he was cute, but what girl doesn't admire the looks of a mixed guy. Miguel's mother was black and his father was Puerto Rican. We asked Aunt Marie about Miguel. She stopped mid stir of her famous potato salad. The look that Aunt Marie gave me over her reading glasses, let me know that I was about to get a lecture.

"He's into drugs and everything now, Roni girl. That boy is bad news! I better not see you outside prancing around". I found interest in something else in the kitchen, to avoid continuation of the unwarranted lecture. Aunt Marie tended to go on and on about a topic. She meant well, but we had heard the same lecture from she and Aunt Chris over and over. Don't talk to boys, they only want one thing. Then my mother would join in with her part of the lecture...

My curiosity was piqued; maybe what I needed was a bad boy. The next day, I set out to get Miguel's attention. Cherry and I found every excuse possible to be outside. We offered to walk to the store, to get stuff out of the car, anything to be seen by Miguel. It wasn't until after Easter dinner that we realized our plan had worked. Miguel had a young sister (Myesha) who came over to ask if we wanted to play with her the next day. Cherry and I giggled at her request, honored that we were now the older kids that little kids wanted to play with. We confirmed our play date and she turned to go back home. She quickly turned back as if she had forgotten something.

"Oh, my brother told me to give this to whoever is oldest". I looked down and saw a note, folded tightly in Myesha's small hand. Thank you! I told her and accepted the note. She turned again, looked both ways and skipped across the street, her wavy black hair telling us goodbye. I opened the letter to find a note scribbled in pen, with a request for "the older sister" to meet at the beginning of the housing development. Cherry nudged me as I read the note and tried to be inconspicuous as our family could be watching us from inside the house. I then devised a plan to sneak out of my aunt's house, to meet a guy that she warned was bad news.

The Easter dinner dishes were washed, and the old folks were sitting around, continuing the conversation about days past. If I timed it right, I could sneak out around 1:30am, if I was back by 5am, when the old folks started stirring again. To my surprise, they were all asleep by 1am. I tapped Cherry that I was leaving before I crept down the hall and climbed out of the bathroom window. I stood still, just to make sure the house wasn't stirring and to let my eyes adjust to the moonlit sky. I had taken a shower and put on my nightclothes (a t-shirt and shorts) after dinner.

The *city* night sky was different from what we had on the Shore. At home, we could see the stars and identify every constellation. Suddenly, I heard something behind me. I turned around to find who I remember as Miguel, but he was a few inches taller than me, with facial hair and his curly hair in a ponytail.

"Miguel?" I asked.

"What up youngin?" he said in a hushed voice. I like the slang that people from D.C. and Prince George's County use. "I ain't seen you in forever. Give me a hug". He grinned, showing a set of gold grills across his top teeth.

I decided to comply with his request. His hug felt good, but awkward. He smelled of something that I wasn't familiar with. (I would learn later that it was called Black and Miles).

"Lemme holla at you. We can go to my boys' house." My gut was telling me this didn't sound like a good idea. But since I was curious, I followed him.

Miguel walked with certainty, but he was looking from side to side... I followed Miguel, intently watching my footsteps as we went across a few streets and a few houses down. I wasn't familiar with where we were exactly, but I knew how to get back to Aunt Marie's if needed. We walked through a backyard that had a gate, and Miguel stopped to look around once more. He walked onto the back porch and opened the back door. The door wasn't locked, and there weren't any lights on. I couldn't tell initially, but the house wasn't occupied. There were remnants that someone had lived there, but no furniture or televisions. I stopped to look around, after I closed the door behind me.

"Come on girl. What you scared?"

"No. But whose house is this?

"Don't worry about it. Don't nobody live here. We can hang out here for a while."

We turned the corner into what I assumed used to be the living room. There were a few bean chairs and a few empty bags leftover from fast food places. I looked around, unsure if I should sit down or make an excuse to leave.

"You aiight? Sit down." he instructed. I slid down onto one of the beanbag chairs.

Miguel tried to make small talk, but his vocabulary was limited. He sparked up a blunt and offered it to me to try. I declined and began to wonder what I was even doing there. I didn't know this guy and my stomach was telling me to get out of there. I guess Miguel noticed my discomfort; he stood up and adjusted his sweatpants that were already sagging.

"I just wonna talk to you. See how you been. Know what I'm saying? But you can leave if you want to." He tried to reassure me.

"Naw you good." I tried to be hip. But I was nervous about what was going to happen next.

Miguel and I spent the next hour talking. I think he was high. He would pause in the middle of the conversation and just stare off. He closed his eyes and smile often.

"I would like to hit that". He commented at one point.

"Oh, for real? What you think I'm a hoe?"

"Naw youngin. I'm just sayin, you look nice in them shorts and everything." He reached over and touched my legs. Then he kinda tapped the outside of my thigh. I grinned, but kinda liked him touching me. I wanted to kiss him; his lips looked nice. I hated the smell of whatever he was smoking, but I was used to kissing Jude who smoked too.

Suddenly, there was a flashlight shining on us from where we had come through the back door.

"Both of you. Turn around and stand up slowly". Said the voice with authority.

I jumped up, looking directly into the light, I was disoriented. I heard Miguel cursing under his breath.

"Just do what they tell you to do." Miguel said out loud, in my direction. I was frozen and not sure what to do. It was the police, a black officer and a white officer. One of the officers walked towards me, grabbed me firmly by the arm and lead me outside to the back yard.

"What's your name, young lady? Where do you live? How do you know Miguel?" I answer all his questions honestly. He was calm and reassuring. I realized that I was shaking, I wanted to cry. I wanted my mother! I told the Officer where Aunt Marie's house was. He informed me that he had to put me in handcuffs and that he would transport me to her house, because I was a minor.

There I was, the good clean church girl in a cop car, in handcuffs at that! What would my mother say? Oh God, what would my grandmother say? Hot tears formed in the corner of my eyes and slid down my cheeks. What was I thinking? I could clearly hear Aunt Marie's warning about Miguel being a bad boy. As we turned the corner to Aunt Marie's house, I could see the time in the cop car, it was 4:30 in the morning. How could I get out of this? What was he going to tell my family?

He parked in front of Aunt Marie's house and came around to my side of the car. He escorted me up to the front door and knocked hard and deliberate, as officers often do. Uncle Bruce was the first to the door, with Aunt Marie and Aunt Chris right on his heels.

"Sorry to bother you sir, Ma'am. Veronica was in an abandoned house with a suspect that we've been watching for some time. The suspect had been breaking into that house for a few months since the previous owners were evicted." The Officer Reported.

By this time, my mother and grandmother had made their way to the front door. The range of emotions that flooded my entire body, most of which was embarrassment. I couldn't pick my head up to face them. I didn't want to see the looks on their faces. Uncle Bruce looked around to see if anyone was watching from the neighborhood. Aunt Marie was a paralegal for a well-known legal defense office in D.C., she didn't need any unwanted gossip to get around where she lived. Uncle Bruce invited the officer into the dining room area. My family members took a seat around the table, while I stood next to the china closet, wishing that I could disappear. The officer informed them that it would be up to the owner of the house if they wanted to press charges. Because I was a minor and didn't have any previous police involvement, I could get off with community service.

That night I prayed differently. I prayed for Miguel, because I didn't know what happened after the officer took me into the back yard. It turned out that he was 22 and he had acquired criminal charges for quite some time. I prayed for the homeowner that they would have mercy on me and not press charges. And I prayed that I would never be arrested; I could still feel the cold metal handcuffs on my wrists. I prayed for my family, that they would forgive me. But would God forgive me? I didn't even know that I needed to forgive myself for what I had allowed myself to get into.

My teenage brain made me believe that I had gotten away with it this time. The homeowners did press charges, but the judge only gave me community service hours. My family looked at me and acted differently toward me, after they saw that I had the propensity to do something like this. I wasn't as innocent as

I had portrayed, getting good grades and being active in church. I was on punishment for a LONG time. Losing the trust of my family weighed heavy on me. I loved them all and I knew they loved me. They felt betrayed mostly. I hoped that one day, our relationship would be restored to the level that it had been.

FOOTSTEPS IN THE DARK

(The Isley Brothers 1977)

My experiences with Jude and Miguel made me think that it was time for me to get a boyfriend, so that I wouldn't be going from man to man. My urge to have sex hadn't diminished, so I thought that if I just have one guy that I could have sex with, that would be best. Of course, I wanted him to be nice looking, to treat me right and all that, but companionship and having sex was my priority.

Senior year was coming to an end, and I was looking at college prospects. My top five included Salisbury University (close to home), UMES (less than 30 miles away), Towson University and Bowie State. Two of those are considered HBCU's and the other were diverse enough for me to get a good college experience. I met with the Guidance Counselor often, to get applications for grants and scholarships. Every week, my mother was signing for me to get more money to support my college career. She made it clear that we had to get good grades to receive funds to pay for college. Within all my excursions with men, I managed to attend school and keep my grades up, I had a part time job, and I was active in church. And by active, I mean that I attended every service, every time the doors were opened, unless I had to work. I was an usher, I counted the offering, attended Sunday School, gave ideas to the Young People's Auxiliary, and emceed entire services. I knew all the jargon, the church lingo and how to present myself as if I was saved and sanctified. If I showed up, had on the proper attire, no one questioned my lifestyle or if I was living right.

My next excursion was with Andrew, I met him at a skating event sponsored by the Salisbury YMCA. I didn't know how to skate, but I wanted to hang out, and a few of my friends were going too. I dragged Cherry along so she could be my sidekick. I wasn't one to talk to guys, they just seemed to find me. I really didn't have a style, but I was one to put together a pair of jeans (rolled and tucked at the ankles), a nice button up blouse (polka dot or some other design) and some patent leather dress shoes or Reebok Classics. This night I adorned a pair of black jeans, a yellow patterned blouse, my Black Classics, gold bamboo earrings and my hair in a classic ponytail (gelled for good measure). I got a ride to the Y, Cherry and I walked in like we owned the place. By the time we got there around 8:30pm, the high school students had all arrived. We didn't know that there would be a crowd that came in around 9:15 who weren't in school anymore. When they started to trickle in, they almost outnumbered the high school crew. I didn't go out much, so if they hadn't graduated from James M. Bennett or hadn't played sports, I didn't recognize many of the *new crew*. Cherry was getting her usual level of attention from the new crew. But she wasn't giving them any play. She always got the most attention when we were out together, but she was sure to tell the guys, they had to have a friend for her big sister. Shortly after the new crew had looked around at the high schoolers, they began to stake out their territory or which girl they were going to talk to. Just before 10pm (curfew was 11pm), three guys walked over to check out Cherry and me. Two of them were cute, the other was okay looking, but all three were dressed to impress. They each adorned an oversized Polo button up and jeans, with some fresh Tennis (probably Nike's). Cherry and I grinned at each other, flattered that they had come our way.

"Excuse me." One of the cute ones said, flashing his gold capped tooth with his smile. "My friend right here wonna holla at you." He motioned from his funny looking homie, then to me. I was flattered, but I wished he was talking for himself, or the other cute one. Anyways, I looked toward the not so cute one and smiled. He seemed shy, but his smile and the way he looked at me let me know that he liked me. Cherry nudged me toward him, while his homeboys coached him to ask me my name.

"Soooo, wh- wh- what's your name?" He managed to ask me, not really looking directly into my eyes, but somewhere between my chin and my waist. He was wringing his hands and kind of rocking side to side.

"Veronica." I responded, with a grin.

"S ssooooo You got a boyfriend?" He asked, this time with less volume in his voice. I guess in case my answer was yes.

"No." I answered, this time with a wider smile. By this time his home boys high fiving him and boosting him up. I could tell that he was trying to remain calm, but his boys were way hyper than he was.

"So, what's your name?" I tried to keep the conversation going.

"Andrew." He said quickly and with a smile, revealing a set of straight white teeth.

I was impressed. Sometimes guys don't take care of their teeth (or their fingernails), they just cover them with gold caps.

"So can you skate?" He asked. He'd probably noticed that Cherry and I hung out on the outside of the rink and held onto the barrier.

"Not really. Can you?"

"So, you wonna skate with me?" He asked, this time more confidently.

"Sure." I responded with spunk. I glanced at Cherry for permission. I was shocked that neither of the cute guys were trying to talk to her. I would find out later that they both gave her their phone numbers.

Andrew and I began our way around the skating rink. I was still cautious and held onto the barrier around the rink. He reached out for my hand; I held his hand back. It felt nice to have an innocent gesture from someone I just met.

"How old are you?" He asked me when we were almost back to our starting point.

"Almost 18" ...sounded better than 17.

"How old are you?"

"I'm 20."

"So where do you go to high school?" I was trying to figure him out.

"South Dorchester." Which was in Cambridge, about 25 miles north of Salisbury.

The conversation went on like this until I noticed Cherry waving at me from the front door. It was 10:50 and our ride was leaving us. The rink closed at 11 and people hung around outside for a while. There would be no hanging around outside for Chanel's daughters.

Looking at Andrew, I explained to him that I had to go home. We exchanged numbers and he reached in for a hug. It was kind of awkward, but we both smiled and waved goodbye as I found the nearest exit to sit down and take my skates off. I couldn't help but smile, as I gave my skates back to the attendant and skipped over to where Cherry was waiting. We did a silly teenage girl squeal and made our way to the car. All of us were talking about the guys who got our phone numbers and vice versa. I looked back at the parking lot and noticed that Andrew got into a car by himself. It looked like an older model car, like the Oldsmobile that my grandparents drove. I couldn't wait until tomorrow so I could call him; I was thinking I should wait for him to call me.

That Saturday morning, Cherry and I made sure we got our chores done by noon, so that we could chill the rest of the day. Chanel required that we clean our rooms, which included washing, folding, and putting away our laundry, vacuuming, dusting if needed. We were each assigned either the kitchen or the bathroom to clean also. Chanel was specific about how she wanted her house clean! We used Pine-Sol, Mr. Clean, and whatever cleaning products, just as she instructed. If she had to come behind us and we hadn't cleaned properly, it was a problem.

"Oh no you don't!" She would say. "Get your hindparts back in here and clean this bathroom/kitchen right! You know *goodness well* that's not how I taught you! You ain't going nowhere until this house is clean!"

I finished cleaning up around 11:30. Just then, the phone rang. Cherry and I both froze. We were in each other's line of vision and neither of us was close to the house phone, which was only in the kitchen and in our mother's bedroom. Not that we weren't allowed to answer the phone, but usually Chanel was the primary phone answerer.

"I wonder who that could be?" She mumbled under her breath. "Hello. God bless you!" This was her greeting for incoming calls. Cherry and I were pretending as if we weren't interested in who was calling the phone.

"You want to talk to who? Veronica? And may I ask who's calling? Andrew? Andrew who? And how do you know my daughter?" By this time Cherry was walking swiftly to her bedroom, trying to hold her laugh in.

"Roni girl, some boy Andrew on the phone. How old are you anyway?" By this time, I was standing next to her, reaching out for the phone, smiling, and hoping that he hadn't responded to her last question.

"Hey Andrew. What's up?" I tried to play it cool. Chanel stood there, trying to figure out what kind of conversation I was having with Andrew. I knew that I couldn't have a prolonged conversation, with my mother standing there monitoring.

"I had a nice time last night." he said in his soft, shy voice.

"I did too." I tried not to smile hard. After all, I didn't know this guy very well. We had only made small talk while I was trying not to fall.

"So, when can I see you again?" I wanted to smile so hard!

"I don't know. I'll let you know later today." I paused because although my mother was in another part of the house, she was surely ear hustling in my phone conversation.

"I gotta go, but what you doing today?" I was trying to get off the phone.

"Me and my homeboys, the ones from last night, we going to Salisbury Mall. Maybe catch a movie or something." The lightbulb turned on over top of my head.

"Oh, aiight then. Maybe I'll see you there," I said. He could probably hear me smiling, but I was trying to remain calm.

"Cool. I hope I see you then. Peace." He ended the call. There was something slick and mature about the way he said "peace". The only other people I heard say that at the end of conversations were my Aunt Christine's friends. Most of them lived in or near D.C. and they were products of the militant 60's.

"Where you thinking you going today young lady?" My mother inquired from her bedroom.

"I was gonna ask you if we could go to the mall later." I knew that Cherry would have to go with me. That was her rule, so that we could keep an eye on each other.

"Oh okay. So, when you gonna ask me?"

"Mom, can we PLEASE go to the mall later?"

And now here come the questions...How ya'll getting there? What time is your curfew? When are you leaving here? What ya'll gonna be doing? What movie ya'll going to see? Who's paying for you to go? This ain't no date! (We weren't officially allowed to date until we were 18). Don't forget your curfew is 11, we got church in the morning! Make sure you represent, like we love the Lord. Jesus is watching you know! Everywhere you go, EVEN at the Mall-young lady.

Why my mother always felt the need to give us the same lecture before we went anywhere, I wouldn't understand until I became a mother. By 3pm Cherry and I were dressed in our best; our friend Corie had agreed to come pick us up and transport us to the mall. She pulled up to our house and came up to the door. Chanel didn't allow anyone to just pull up, honk their horn and we go outside to their car. She said the respectful thing to do was for them to at least come to the door. When Corie knocked on the front door, I opened it to let her in and my mother gave her the once over to make sure she was dressed appropriately. Although our church preferred that we wear skirts or dresses, our mother said it was okay for us to wear jeans if we were going to the mall to hang out. Corie went to church with us. Her parents knew our mother, so she trusted her to take us there and bring us home. We weren't allowed to wear anything tight or revealing, so jeans and t-shirts it was. I couldn't WAIT until I was 18 and out on my own, so I could wear whatever I wanted to! Of course, our earrings, bracelets and accessories were part of the outfit, Cherry and I had ours matching. It was almost April, so we took our jean jackets just in case it got cooler that night. Sometimes after the movies, we stood outside and hung out until there was just enough time for us to get home by curfew.

We left Chanel's house, under her careful watch, looking one way. But when we stepped out of Corie's car at the mall, we all had slightly modified our attire. I put on a belt that pulled in my waistline and I changed my t-shirt to a blouse that better accentuated my C cups. Cherry had a hair tie that she used to tie her t-shirt in the back, which showed off her small waist and curves. Corie was a full D cup and she had hips which exemplified the hourglass figure. She had on a jean skirt that she rolled under at the hem and pulled up to just under her breasts. She also had on a bodysuit under her t-shirt, so she removed the t-shirt and relieved all her endowed *breasteses*, putting me and Cherry to shame! Corie had also brought lipstick for us to wear. We weren't allowed to wear makeup either, but we had red lips that night!

We strutted into that mall like our names were on the front of it! You couldn't tell us nothing!! Corie smiled as if we had just pulled off an international heist! Unless we saw someone from our church, our parents wouldn't know that we were out in public trying to look grown. By the time we walked through Boscov's into the main mall area, the crowds of teenagers and young adults were scarce. The movie area was crowded, but we wanted to see who all was at the mall! We began to walk the length of the mall, looking around like we were royalty. I was looking for Andrew, but I knew if I didn't see him, there would be other sights for me. I spoke too soon, we were almost to *Claire's* jewelry store when I heard, "There go your girl yo! Go talk to her!"

Corie, Cherry and I all turned around to see a group of the guys from the skating rink. Andrew was walking straight toward me, full speed ahead. He almost ran into a small child; he was so focused on getting to me. As he got closer, he seemed to be getting shorter. But the time he was standing in front of me, it was quite evident that he was at least 4 inches shorter than me. Dang it!! I didn't notice the night before because we were both wearing skates. Cherry glanced my way, with a strained look on her face. She knew I had a thing for guys who were taller than me. To have to look down at a guy I like makes me feel like he can't protect me. I forced a smile and a "Whassup".

He was cheesing real hard and his boys were checking out Corie, trying to figure out who she was. Andrew spoke with Cherry and introduced himself to Corie. Okay, great...he has manners. He asked if I wanted to walk with him to the food court.

"Yeah, that's cool." I looked over at Cherry and Corie. They gave me the head nod of approval. "Where ya'll gonna be at?" I asked them.

"I'm not sure, we'll find you though. Cherry reassured me.

"Okay then cool. I see ya'll later". I turned back to Andrew, and we proceeded to walk toward the food court. "I could use one of those chinese food combos right about now." I hinted to Andrew. As we moseyed on down to the food court, I could see groups of teens who were standing or walking themselves looking at Andrew and me. Some guys would walk up and give him a pound, give me the up-down and keep it moving. Other groups would just stare or just look at us like "who did we think we were? By the time we got to the food court, I could see that the line to the Chinese food place was long, but the line for

Annie's only had three people. I said out loud, so he could hear me, "Oooooh, I want some snickerdoodles".

"Oh, for real! How many?" He said, while reaching into his back pocket. Before I could say anything else, he was in Annie's line, ready to place an order. "You want something to drink too?" I hadn't even answered the first question.

"I'll take 3 Snickerdoodles and a lemonade."

"Okay, that's it?"

"Yeah". I couldn't help but grin. I looked around the food court for a place to sit. He paid for my order and followed me to a nearby table.

By 9:30, we had walked the length of the mall at least 8 times. We would sit and talk, then walk and talk and then sit again. I saw Cherry and Corie a few times and we would ask what each other was doing. I told Andrew that my curfew was 11. He asked if he could drive me home. That was okay with me because I was tired of the mall scene and wanted to be alone with Andrew. I wasn't physically attracted to him. But because he made me smile, he was polite, courteous and didn't ask dumb questions, I was finding myself liking him more. I found Cherry and Corie and told them that I was leaving with Andrew. We had to time this right so that our mother wouldn't know that I was leaving with Andrew. Also, we had to change back into our proper outfits, and I couldn't forget to wipe off the lipstick that I had applied.

Andrew led me to the nearest exit, and we walked across the parking lot. When we got to his car, (I remembered it from the night before, it was a dark blue 1988 Delta Oldsmobile) he opened the passenger door for me to get in. I could get used to this kind of chivalry. We drove around Salisbury as if it were a metropolis and we had a lot to look at. He turned onto the campus of Salisbury University and parked in a parking lot with little lighting.

"I had a nice time with you." he said

"We didn't do anything but walk around." I laughed. "Thanks for buying my food by the way."

"That's what a man supposed to do." He paused, as if he wanted to say more. And he did, "I like you a lot." He paused again, looked out of the windshield, and looked back at me. "I'm wondering if you'll be my girl.".

Shock and awe.

"But you just met me". Was all that I could come up with. The look on his face was of disappointment. "I'm not saying no."

I tried to correct myself. "I'm just saying we should get to know each other better".

"Oh okay, that's cool. Well, when you have an answer, will you let me know." He reached over and held my hand. He rubbed it gently and his hand went up to my shoulder. Before I knew it, he was pulling my arm toward him and leaning in for a kiss. It was nice, gentle. His mouth tasted like the Bazooka gum that he was chewing. He leaned back, as if to look at my face for approval. I smiled so he leaned in again. That night we did a lot of kissing and leaning back, until I noticed the digital clock in his car read 10:45. We weren't that far away from my house

"You gonna give me an answer tomorrow right?" He reminded me that I hadn't answered his question yet.

"Yeah."

"Yeah, you'll be my girl or yeah you'll give me an answer."

I laughed. "Yeah, I'll give you an answer."

He turned onto the street where I lived, and I showed him where to park. I untucked my t-shirt and made sure the lipstick was gone. I made him turn his lights off just in case Chanel was looking out of the kitchen window (as she often did). Corie was parked, waiting for me to get in so that Cherry and I could both get out of the car together. I got out of Andrews car and walked swiftly to Corie's car, so that she could pull up in front of our house, as if I were with her and not Andrew.

When we walked into the house, Chanel was waiting, sitting on the living room couch. She gave us the once over, turned off the TV and went to her room. We went into our bedroom so that, Cherry and I could talk in detail about the day's happenings. I told her that Andrew had asked me to be his girl. Her eyes got big and she covered her mouth so that she could stop herself from screaming!

"What did you say?"

"I told him I would give him an answer tomorrow".

"Why you do that?" She said, giving me a nudge.

"Because yo, I don't know him like that! I can tell he really likes me though. He bought me snickerdoodles girl! You know how much I LOVE me some snickerdoodles!!" I laid back on my bed with excitement.

The next day, I couldn't wait to call Andrew, after church. I gave him my answer, which was yes, I'd be his girl. Over the next few days, Andrew and I spent a lot of time together. We usually met up at the mall, or some other public place. The next weekend, he told me about his job and that he had rented a room in Hurlock from an older lady that he knew growing up. Andrew was a man. He wasn't like Jude, who seduced and took advantage of a teenage girl.

Within two weeks, Andrew invited me to his apartment. The lady he lived with was going out of town. I had to devise a scheme to get out of the house to his apartment, which was about 15 miles away. Growing up, Chanel didn't allow us to spend the night at or to even visit our friends' houses. "I don't know them people like that!" She would always say. Although we were dang near adults!

That weekend, I was so nervous! I had never spent the night at a guy's house. I told myself that this was okay because Andrew was my boyfriend. I hadn't had sex in almost a month. I was sure that we were going to have sex, so I made sure that I shaved the proper areas and that I wore my best underwear. I snuck out of the house on a Friday night and walked around to where Andrew was waiting to pick me up, around the corner. He was wearing a t-shirt and sweatpants with his smile was extra wide.

That night I found out the true meaning of a Mandingo. Andrew was well endowed, but he took his time and made sure that I was comfortable. I couldn't believe how big it was! He asked me often if I was okay. He knew what he was working with and wanted to make sure that he wasn't hurting me! I had questions...how did it get that big? How was it bigger than Jude's? How many girls had he been with, and could they take **all** that he had to offer? We had sex twice that night, and he held me until it was time for me to go home around 5:30 a.m.

Chanel was an earlier riser, especially on Sunday's. He kissed me intensely, before I got out of his car and made my way to try to sneak back into the house. Cherry met me at our back door, and we tipped quietly to our respective rooms. How she knew when I was coming, I don't know, but she always had my back! I had to wait to tell her all the details of my night with Andrew. I moved in slow motion that day, I couldn't wait to get back home and lay down. I told my mother it was because my period was coming. This was true. Andrew used condoms, so I wasn't concerned that I was pregnant.

Was I a hoe? Would God forgive me? I hadn't forgiven myself!! Did I understand the consequences of having sexual partners for the wrong reasons? Andrew and I kept dating and having sex for almost a year. That's until I had a greater life lesson to learn in realizing how valuable my life, time and family meant to me.

GRANDMA'S HANDS

(Bill Withers, 1971)

A t the <u>beginning of my senior year in high school,</u> the whispering began. My family was talking a lot, about something they didn't want Cherry and I to hear. They called our mother often and she took the calls, speaking in hushed tones so we couldn't hear her. I couldn't quite gather exactly what, but something was wrong with pop pop, but they wouldn't tell us specifically. I could observe his weakness, not quite being himself, his complexion was different, and he didn't leave the house as much.

"Poppop has Cancer." Uncle Bruce broke the news to us that October.

Cancer, I thought to myself. But I just sat there. Still. Confused. Unsure of the magnitude of the news that Uncle

Bruce had just shared with me about my hero. The living room seemed like it was closing in around me. I looked around at the 1970's paneled walls, looked toward my grandmother for assurance and to my mother who was barely holding herself together. Just hearing the word, cancer, struck fear and panic that I couldn't understand. There were commercials on television about organizations raising money for cancer treatment, but what did this mean for *my* Poppop? My grandfather and I had a special bond as far back as I can remember. He even gave me a nickname, *Sqwaziemoe*. He called me that because he said that when I was born, I looked like an Indian. Needless to say, he knew nothing of being politically correct.

I knew very little about cancer. My paternal grandfather had cancer and passed away when Cherry and I were in elementary school. Even at that time, we weren't told that he died from cancer. It just kind of slipped out during a conversation with my dad, several years AFTER my paternal grandfather had passed away. So, did that mean that my maternal grandfather was now going to pass away too?

During the following 11 months, there were doctor's visits, family conversations about his care and treatment, hospital stays, surgery to remove gallstones and then hospice care. I didn't understand any of it and we were still not allowed to ask questions about "grown folks business". I always knew that my grandparents would pass away one day, but this wasn't fair. He needed to be at my high school graduation, sitting on the front row (with that stern look) at my wedding ceremony and to hold his great grandchildren.

My grandfathers were both respected in the community as stand-up men, who were honest, family oriented and who provided for their family. They were both active in ministry at their respective churches. They were always present, not in a lovey dovey playful sense, but in a stern, meek and humble sense. I watched my maternal poppop arrive at church before everyone else, stayed for the duration of how many services we had, cleaned up and locked the doors after everyone else left. He was a tall, dark skinned slip man who walked with a pep in his step, until the rainy weather troubled his *bad leg*. The story is that someone was cutting grass and the blade came off and went into his leg; he didn't receive proper medical treatment, so it didn't heal properly. Unfortunately, I wasn't as close to my paternal grandfather, simply because my parents were separated, and we didn't see our paternal grandparents often. I do remember he was short, had dark caramel skin, wore black framed glasses, and drove a white Dodge Plymouth hatchback with red stripes.

Another similarity that I noticed with my grandparents was their skin. They were beautiful shades of tan, copper, caramel, and mocha. This was amazing to me, as I looked at the spectrum of brown faces within my family. My mother, with her light skin and freckles, my father with his dark chocolate hue and reddish-brown hair, came together to create me, caramel with hints of red and Cherry, almond colored with hints of orange. I remember being fascinated with my grandmothers' hands. Their fingers were thick enough to wring out clothes they'd washed by hand, gentle enough to part hair and grease a scalp, yet powerful enough to pop the seal from a jar of preserves they'd sealed months ago. I'd sit next to them in church and compare my small, smooth skinned hands, to their chubby hands that were lined, ingrained with years of raising children and manual labor.

My grandmothers' hands meant comfort, strength, and healing. Neither of them ever told me that they loved me. But I could tell by the way they allowed me to fall asleep on their arm or with my head in their lap. I could tell when they told me to go get the comb and some grease (Blue Bergamont or Dax), and then instructed me to grease their scalp. I could tell the way they wore their Sunday hats and clapped their hands during service, and they'd look down at me to make sure that I was okay.

After the news that poppop had cancer, I kept thinking, poppop can't die! Who would carve the Thanksgiving turkey? Who would go with me to buy my first car and tell me when it needed to be fixed? He was an all-around handyman; when anything needed to be fixed, they would call MY poppop. It was like he had on a cape under his church suit or the jumper that he wore when he was working on kerosene stoves or fixing cars, chopping wood or gardening. Not to mention that he could cook, he could clean a house from top to bottom, he could braid hair and sew his own button back on his shirt.

They don't make 'em like my grandparents anymore! My paternal grandmother raised her own children and then provided foster care for more than 40 children in the community. She was an excellent seamstress, she made fruit preserves and she could cook a meal to feed the entire neighborhood. Although I wasn't a fan of her chitterlings (yuck), her homemade yeast rolls and sweet potato pies would make you wonna slap your mother! She could crochet blankets that kept us warm when we would visit her house. She taught me how to crochet a chain stitch and I learned how to sew in

Home Economics Class. I was so proud when I showed her my first creation, a pair of shorts that I could wear to gym class. I didn't realize during those times that the art of sewing, and cooking would be diminished with the expansion of fashion designers who just wanted their names on the tag and using microwaveable meals. Life seemed to move faster when my grandmothers passed away. I wish that I had taken the time to learn more about them. Now all I have is stories, pictures, and some of the blankets they created.

I remember the day that poppop passed away. The night before, the family gathered around his hospital bed that hospice care had placed in the living room. I remember Aunt Marie rubbing his arm and singing a few of his favorite hymns to him. Then she said to poppop, "It's okay Daddy, if you're tired, you can go". I couldn't believe she said that! I ran to my bedroom, confused and feeling hopeless. The next morning, the house and the outside were eerily quiet. They had a dog that ALWAYS barked, for no reason, really. I looked out of the bedroom window and the dog was outside, seated inside of his house, quietly. This was TOO weird, and I knew something had to be wrong. I creeped downstairs, listening for voices, and hoping for the smell of bacon and eggs. I had to go through the living room,

I looked over at the bed where he lay and knew that he wasn't there anymore. Aunt Marie quickly redirected me, I saw the look on my mother's face and knew that poppop had "gone to glory" as they say. I ran past everyone and went outside. The dog was the only being who could comfort me. Hospice and the funeral director came shortly. I watched from the yard, the dog and I, trying to make sense of it all.

The Homegoing Service for poppop was truly a celebration. In our church, we didn't mourn the loss of family members in a dreaded somber manner. We celebrate their life, their achievements and their "going home to be with the Lord". Don't get me wrong, we were sad, but we didn't dwell on the loss of the person. Rather, we believe we will see them again, in heaven. We wore white attire, sang upbeat songs, and told memorable stories of the recently departed.

After the homegoing service, I had a lot of unanswered questions about life and death. Although he was a great minister of the gospel, I wondered about what seemed to be contradictions of the Word of God and the plight of the People of Color that I saw daily. My grandparents weren't the militant type who talked about race, but their actions taught me that People of Color were seen as inferior. They used terms like

"Colored" and "them vs. us", as it relates to White and Black people. I watched my poppop as a revered minister at Sunday Service, and as a seemingly weak, spineless *Stepin Fetchit* character, for the White folks throughout the week.

How could such a loving God allow People of Color to suffer such atrocities as the Atlantic Slave Trade, slavery and blatant racism in the United States? The original Jim Crow and the *new* Jim Crow with its' economic inequalities, systemic racist practices; the so-called "War on Drugs" and mass incarceration, I found no resolve for in the Bible. How could a God who is merciful and just, look down on us and not intervene on our plight? How could such a loving God not make things better for our people? After all, we are kings and queens, business owners, engineers (The Pyramids), mathematicians (NASA), Inventors and medical innovators (Dr. James McCune Smith, Dr. Charles Richard Drew). We were stolen from our Native Land, and taken to a stolen land, then made to build a country that wouldn't consider us as equal without legislation.

Cancer stole my grandfathers, and so many more of that generation who were oppressed and therefore suppressed their true feelings about their perceived status in life. They were just trying to get ahead! They wanted the American Dream, to find love, to raise children and to leave a legacy for the next generation. Why couldn't they get ahead? They worked hard, instilled value and morals into their children, paid their taxes and operated in respect and honesty. But the system wasn't made for *US* to prosper.

Racism stole my voice, my confidence and my trust in a system that's supposed to protect and serve. It taught me that you could succumb to a system that you were kidnapped into. You could assimilate into that system and still be regarded as less than who God created you to be. Racial inequalities and health disparities could kill you before you had the ability to see your great grandchildren or even make 80 years of age.

Make no mistake, my trust, my hope, and my resolve are in God. The Creator of the Universe is eternal, He is Love, He is Just, and I trust Him! So, with this, I am confident in Romans 8:28 And we know [with great confidence] that God [who is deeply concerned about us] causes all things to work together [as a plan] for good for those who love God, to those who are called according to His plan and purpose (Amplified version). That's what faith is after all, believe what we can't yet see (Hebrews 11:1).

A DIFFERENT WORLD

(Theme song by Aretha Franklin, 1989-1993)

One of my favorite television shows of the late 80s and early 90s, is *A Different World*. The sitcom aired from 1987-1993 and was based on the life of students at a Historically Black College/University (HBCU). On the campus of Hillman College, Denise Huxtable, Dwayne Wayne, Whitley Gilbert, Jaleesa Vinson, and the other characters confronted many challenges and addressed common social concerns of the time. Although Hillman is a fictional college, the show accurately depicted the Black response to social ills that plagued our community, including HIV/AIDS, the Los Angeles Riots, and the Black experience in America.

When I received my acceptance letter to attend Bowie State, I couldn't have been prouder to become among the elite of an HBCU. Bowie State, established in 1865 by and for previously enslaved peoples, has produced numerous accomplished actors, politicians, and educators. And now I would be attending an institute of higher learning, where many staff and students look like me, my family, and our ancestry. I arrived on campus, bright eyed and full of high hopes and expectations. My major was Pre-Medicine, with a minor in childhood studies. I had always wanted to be a pediatrician, influenced by Dr. Huxtable on the Cosby Show. I packed all my worldly possessions, new sheets and toiletries into my borrowed footlocker from Aunt Candy.

My first day on campus, I was nervous and excited about the possibilities of this institute of higher learning. I had to set an example for my sister and younger cousins. I was raised on working 10 times harder to prove myself as a Black woman. Greeted by the Bowie mascot (Bulldog) and groups of Black and Brown faces, I was mesmerized by shades of melanin that filled the campus. Intricate hairstyles, head coverings and families helping students move into their dormitories named after Black heroes.

Aunt Marie picked me up from Salisbury early that Saturday in August and we were on our way to Bowie, MD. Getting my room assignment from the Bursar's Office, we drove around to Harriett Tubman Hall. I couldn't believe that I would be living in a dorm named for a Black woman who freed enslaved people and then became a spy for the Union Army! I was so excited, and I felt empowered to be living in Tubman Hall. I climbed the steps with the first load of my belongings, knocked on the door and was greeted by two cheerful roommates who introduced themselves as cousins. I found out that night that Ama and Ashanti were originally from Accra, Ghana. We got to know each other that weekend, as they asked questions about the Eastern Shore, and I certainly had questions about their place of origin. I was honestly jealous that they could point on a map where they were from, and they spoke several languages. They lived in Montgomery County locally and their work/school ethic were outstanding. They worked full time jobs, studied ALL the time AND were nursing majors.

Fortunately, I knew one person on campus, Lucy who was from Silver Springs. She was a friend of a friend, and I would come to know that she knew EVERYONE. She is also from Ghana, by way of Montgomery County. Lucy is a statuesque athlete, and an avid listener of music, especially Go Go. She was always in the know, dragging me along to campus events and to events at Towson State, UMBC and Morgan State (Shanda was our connection there). Between Lucy and my roommates, they introduced my pallet to Ghanaian inspired dishes, including jollof rice. They wore waist beads, adorned headwraps and different kinds of jewelry (wooden, colorful pieces like Aunt Christine work). I became fascinated as they introduced me to their culture, and I couldn't help but wonder if my ancestors were captured and passed through the Elmina Castle on the coast of Ghana.

One thing that Bowie has, like Salisbury, is a diverse demographic. Salisbury, however, is rural and diverse because of its agricultural base (farming and factories employ migrant workers from Haiti and Mexico for example). Bowie is nestled in Prince George's County, which is known for having upper class Black families. Nahum, who lived in Bowie, (his parents were originally from Senegal), introduced himself to me at the first Black Student Union event. He also shared that he studied Islam, which I didn't know much about. He was friendly but I could tell that he was focused on his studies and wasn't looking to be in a relationship. I was fascinated with him, especially because of his skin tone, it looked burnt by the sun, but well moisturized and it glistened when he sweat. I was also fascinated during our conversations, that although my mother is African American and his mother is Senegalese, they had similar sayings, rules and what not. I wondered how two different women, from different origins and with different life experiences, had raised their children in such similar fashions. My conversations with Nahum taught me how naive I truly was, especially about the African and Black diaspora. Stories from my Aunt Christine's travels and the We Are the World collaboration were the extent of what I knew about Africa. Nahum helped me realize that I needed to do more research on my own, about Africa, about Black people in the United States and elsewhere and to talk with other Black people about their black experiences. History class in high school, didn't teach me about the events that brought my ancestors to the Eastern Shore and so forth. So, I began to search for knowledge, not just about being Black, but I still wanted to understand the roots of Christianity and how it is applicable as time moves on.

While doing laundry one day, I met Chris, who was the Resident Assistant for Tubman Hall. He was cute and athletic, from being on the Row Team. He seemed kind, but also came off as cocky. I introduced him to Lucy at a soccer game. She agreed about the cuteness, but also observed that he seemed to be controlling. I would find out in the second semester that he had a girlfriend that he didn't keep his hands off of. Not because he loved her, but because he was really controlling, to the point that he would hit her, and she was seen in class with bruises on her face and arms. I didn't know his girlfriend, but when I heard from a reliable source that Chris was abusive, I kept my distance from that point on. I wasn't sure how to respond or if I could help the girlfriend in any way. The term domestic violence wasn't part of my vocabulary. I hadn't seen what I observed to be physical, emotional, or verbal abuse, when I was growing up.

My first year at Bowie, Lucy introduced me to so many people, from her basketball team, from her dorm and just random people that she became friends with. I began to learn more and more about who I was and who I wanted to be. Bowie was becoming a great experience for this naive country girl. One experience that I wished hadn't happened, was with my friend Andrice. We met at a Black Student Union event, she was from Snow Hill, which is near Salisbury. Andrice was shy like me, but she had a boyfriend at Bowie; they knew each other from high school. One night, after an event at UMBC, we went to

Andrice's boyfriend's apartment, he lived off campus. He was part of a fraternity and some of his frat brothers joined us to hang out. They brought alcohol and some recreational drugs for those who chose to indulge. The hour grew later, but we were having fun, watching Martin, listening to Bob Marley, laughing, and enjoying each other's company. I didn't like the taste of beer and there was enough marijuana in the air for a significant contact. Andrice's boyfriend on the other hand was drinking and smoking like there was no tomorrow! At some point after midnight, some other guys who weren't students but lived in the apartment building, joined the gathering. Andrice wanted to spend the night, so we all dozed off wherever we landed in the living room or otherwise. Around 4am, I got up to use the bathroom. I quietly stepped over everyone where they lay, and I heard some commotion coming from the bedroom. I wasn't alarmed, until I heard what sounded like a slap and a muffled wince. I walked toward the bedroom and the sound intensified. I called out to Andrice and walked into the bedroom.

What I saw next haunted me for years into my adulthood. I screamed to get the attention of someone else to help. Without thought, I lunged toward the bed, to help Andrice. One of the guys that I really didn't know, had Andrice pinned to the bed with his hand covering her mouth. She looked at me in despair as he was trying to take off her panties. Others from the living room came into the bedroom to help. The girls comforted Andrice, as the guys took the perpetrator outside to give him a proper beatdown. Andrice chose to press charges, so that she could feel safe when visiting her boyfriend. Andrice wasn't quite the same after this. She didn't want to hang out and her relationship with her boyfriend was strained.

During orientation, the student ambassadors warned us about date rape. I hadn't heard this term before, but they described it as when you know someone, and they sexually assault the acquaintance. Andrice shared with us that she had met the perpetrator a few times when she visited her boyfriends' apartment. She tried to blame herself for the incident and her boyfriend blamed himself for getting drunk and smoking. I tried to be supportive, but I didn't know how to. We kept in touch until our Senior year. She left college and took a paid internship in Annapolis.

My relationship with my high school boyfriend Daniel, didn't stay steady while I was at Bowie. He went to attend Salisbury University and we saw each other when I came home to visit. I wasn't really looking for another boyfriend while I was on campus. But I would meet someone during Bowie Homecoming that would change my life forever. Thomas Brown was a senior; he was like a celebrity on campus. I saw girls swooning around him at every event. I just knew that he was probably having sex with all of them. There were rumors around campus about Thomas, how well-endowed he was and if you had sex with him, you couldn't walk for a day or two. I had to admit, he was gorgeous, mocha skin with a chiseled body, wavy hair, and a nice smile. Apparently, I caught his eye, because of all the girls around him, he came to dance with me. Somewhere in between Award Tour by A Tribe Called Quest and Woo Hah! Got You All In Check, by Busta Rhymes, I found myself liking Thomas. He had this cocky swag about him, and I was sucked in by his city boy charm. We began to date, and our conversations involved making plans together beyond our college years.

My college experience taught me more about the Black diaspora in four years that I had learned in my first 18 years of life.

DELIVER ME (THIS IS MY EXODUS)

(Donald Lawrence & The Tri-City Singers, feat. Leandria Johnson, 2019)

T he Color Purple is one of my favorite movies. The stories of the characters are relatable, although the era was decades before my time. Just like Miss Celie, I had suffered abuse at the hands of men who were broken themselves. I had also found myself at the hands of teenagers and young adults who had to know that what they were doing was wrong. How else could a individual abuse anyone, unless they've been abused themselves?

Dear God,

Please don't let this one hurt me, like the others have. I just want to love him and to be loved by him. No games, no fear, no meaningless sex.

Who am I as a result of all that's happened to me? I don't understand all that's happened to me. I have suppressed so much, sometimes the experiences run together. I hope that I don't become like those broken men and hurt others. I hope that I can one day become a wife and a good mother.

*****

Four years after graduating from Bowie...

I loved Thomas Brown, but I knew it was a mistake to have married him. Now with two sons and our third child (hopefully a girl) on the way, I felt that I had to stay with him. I had convinced myself that he would change. The love I had for my son's was more than I could have imagined and I thought they needed their father in their lives. Thomas' kind of love satisfied my body but hurt my heart and left my mind empty. I hoped that he would fulfill my longing for the love that I knew was available, from someone, I just hadn't met them yet. I hoped that if we had a little girl, Thomas would love me better and not hurt my heart as much.

As I sat one Sunday in July at St. James' Church, tears began to roll down my face as I heard Pastor Nathans preach about forgiveness. Being in church all my life, now an adult, married, with a college degree, I have never heard anyone explain it in this manner. It was like a dam had broken and hot salty tears flowed from my tear ducts.

"Forgiveness releases you, not the other person", Pastor Nathans explained. "We don't forgive because the other person asks for forgiveness. We forgive because that's the Christlike thing to do."

I don't remember the scripture that he used or much more of the sermon, I just knew that statement pierced my heart, and I began to weep, uncontrollable. At first the tears were of anger, then of confusion and why I had to forgive.

It all came back...my first glimpse of a penis, Cherry telling me that James made her touch his penis, the Brute and Oriole cap of Deacon Thomas, sleeping with boyfriend after boyfriend, trying to fill a void. I thought about my real reason for wanting to get married and now my feeling inadequate as a wife and mother. I wept for my children and I hoped they wouldn't have to go through what I did as a child and teenager. I vowed to protect them at all cost. I thought about those who had gathered along with me at this church and other places of worship, who had been abused by "good people". I wept for those who couldn't tell their parents, family members or any trusted adult, because they didn't think it would help them. I wept for those who experienced sexual trauma and turned to unhealthy coping skills as adults. And I wept for anyone that I knew personally who was still trapped in abusive sexual exchanges or who were being sexually exploited in any way.

My face tingled, my limbs fell loose, and it was as if I was now alone in the edifice is of 800 or more members. I could hear Pastor Nathans continuing with his sermon, members responding with Amens and Hallelujahs, but I could also feel the warmth of something I couldn't explain. I had experienced the power of the Holy Spirit on many occasions, but this was renewing, refreshing and personal. I could feel that someone had gently placed a wad of tissues in my hand and was gently rubbing my back. When I finally wept my last cleansing tear, I was bent forward into the bench in front of me. Sis. Addison was sitting in the pew in front of me, with her reassuring and warm smile. I looked around, rubbed my swelling belly and breathed a heavy sigh of relief. Tanya was sitting nearby with Daniel and Thomas Jr, their father was in the media room as he often was after service. I felt different, as if a weight was lifted and my head was clear. I could be a good wife, an excellent mother and walk in the gifts that God has given me. It didn't matter what had been stolen from me, I could be restored by the power of the living God!

Made in the USA
Middletown, DE
09 November 2021

51951771R00071